DISCARDED

Justin Bieber

kid STARS!

Gillian Gosman

PowerKiDS press
New York

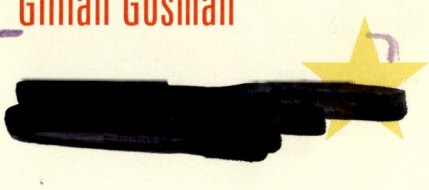

Published in 2012 by The Rosen Publishing Group, Inc.
29 East 21st Street, New York, NY 10010

Copyright © 2012 by The Rosen Publishing Group, Inc.

All rights reserved. No part of this book may be reproduced in any form without permission in writing from the publisher, except by a reviewer.

First Edition

Editor: Jennifer Way
Book Design: Kate Laczynski
Layout Design: Julio Gil

Photo Credits: Cover Michael Buckner/WireImage/Getty Images; p. 4 Bryan Bedder/Getty Images; p. 7 Larry Busacca/Getty Images for NARAS; p. 8 Frazer Harrison/Getty Images; p. 11 Jason Merritt/Getty Images; p. 12 Mike Stobe/Getty Images; p. 15 Alexander Tamargo/Getty Images; p. 16 Neilson Barnard/Getty Images; p. 19 Kevin Winter/Getty Images; p. 20 Kevin Mazur/VF11/WireImage/Getty Images.

Library of Congress Cataloging-in-Publication Data

Gosman, Gillian.
 Justin Bieber / by Gillian Gosman. — 1st ed.
     p. cm. — (Kid stars!)
 Includes index.
 ISBN 978-1-4488-6190-3 (library binding) — ISBN 978-1-4488-6339-6 (pbk.) —
ISBN 978-1-4488-6340-2 (6-pack)
 1. Bieber, Justin, 1994—-Juvenile literature. 2. Singers—Canada—Biography—Juvenile literature. I. Title.
 ML3930.B54G67 2012
 782.42164092—dc23
 [B]
                                         2011019526

Manufactured in the United States of America

CPSIA Compliance Information: Batch #WW12PK: For Further Information contact Rosen Publishing, New York, New York at 1-800-237-9932

Contents

Meet Justin Bieber 5
Justin's Childhood 6
YouTube Star 9
Discovered! 10
My World 13
Bieber Fever 14
My World 2.0 17
Never Say Never 18
Bieber Offstage 21
Fun Facts 22
Glossary 23
Index 24
Web Sites 24

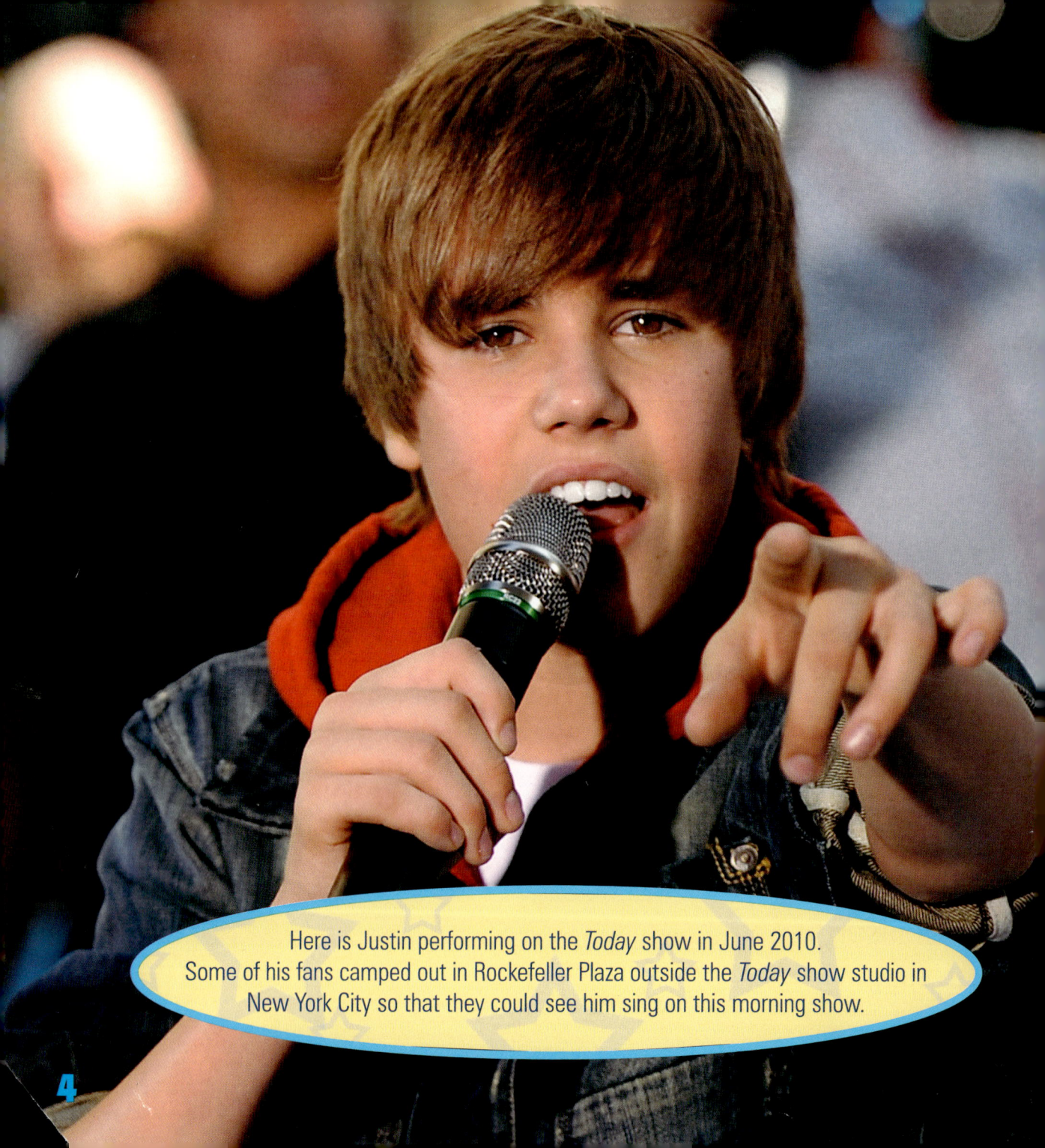

Here is Justin performing on the *Today* show in June 2010. Some of his fans camped out in Rockefeller Plaza outside the *Today* show studio in New York City so that they could see him sing on this morning show.

Meet Justin Bieber

Justin Bieber sings. He taught himself to play guitar, piano, and the trumpet. He plays the drums, too. He also acts. He is a teen star with amazing **talent** and charm. His fans call themselves Beliebers, people who believe in the greatness of Justin Bieber.

Justin's music is pop with plenty of R & B, or rhythm and blues, sound. He sings about young love, setting goals, and growing up. All the while, he is growing up himself! Justin has been compared to superstars such as Michael Jackson, Stevie Wonder, and Ne-Yo. Get ready to learn more about this kid star!

Justin's Childhood

Justin was born on March 1, 1994. He grew up in the small city of Stratford, Ontario, Canada, with his mother, Pattie Mallette. The family did not have much money. As a boy, Justin enjoyed playing soccer and chess.

When Justin was 12, he began singing and playing the guitar on the street. People walking by dropped change into his open guitar case. This is called **busking**. He would busk near the Stratford Festival Theatre. This is a theater that is famous for its popular summer theater festival. In one summer busking there, Justin earned $3,000!

Here is Justin with his mother, Pattie Mallette, at the Grammy Awards in 2010. He was nominated for two Grammys that year.

Scooter Braun (left) found Justin's YouTube videos by accident. He has worked with Justin from the beginning of his career.

YouTube Star

When he was 12, Justin took part in a local talent contest called Stratford Idol. Though he had never had a singing lesson, he won second place in the contest.

Justin had a video taken of his **performance** so that he could share his singing with family and friends. He posted the video of his performance on YouTube, a video-sharing Web site. The video went **viral**. This means that not only family and friends, but also lots of strangers started watching his videos. Over the next year, he posted more videos of himself singing, and soon those videos went viral, too.

Discovered!

One of the people who saw Justin's early YouTube videos was an Atlanta-based **manager** named Scott "Scooter" Braun. He thought Justin was a talented singer. In 2008, he invited Justin to visit him in Atlanta, Georgia, and to record a few songs in a real recording studio. It was Justin's first trip out of Canada.

Not long after, music star Usher saw one of Justin's videos, too. Usher could see that Justin had great talent and the drive to succeed. Usher took Justin under his wing. Usher and Braun helped Justin get a **recording deal** with Island Records. Next thing they knew, Justin and his mom were moving to Atlanta.

Usher (left) has been a mentor to Justin. Here they are at the 2010 American Music Awards. Between the two of them, they won five American Music Awards that year!

My World included the four great singles "One Time," "One Less Lonely Girl," "Love Me," and "Favorite Girl." Here is Justin singing a song from that album on *Good Morning America* in 2009.

My World

In July 2009, Island Records **released** Justin's first single, "One Time." In November of that year, the record company released Justin's first full album, *My World*. For the album, Justin had the chance to work with some of the best songwriters and **music producers** in the business.

To **promote**, or sell, the album, Justin began touring the United States, Canada, and the United Kingdom. His work paid off. The album went **platinum** in the United States, which means it sold one million copies. It went double platinum in Canada and Great Britain, meaning it sold two million copies.

Bieber Fever

In 2009, Justin's music **career** really began to take off! That year, he performed on television talk shows around the world. He even performed for President Barack Obama and First Lady Michelle Obama at the White House as part of the television event *Christmas in Washington*. Soon after, he performed on *Dick Clark's New Year's Rockin' Eve with Ryan Seacrest*.

Justin Bieber was now a household name. His fans said that they had "Bieber Fever." Justin welcomed the attention. He knew he wanted to be a star.

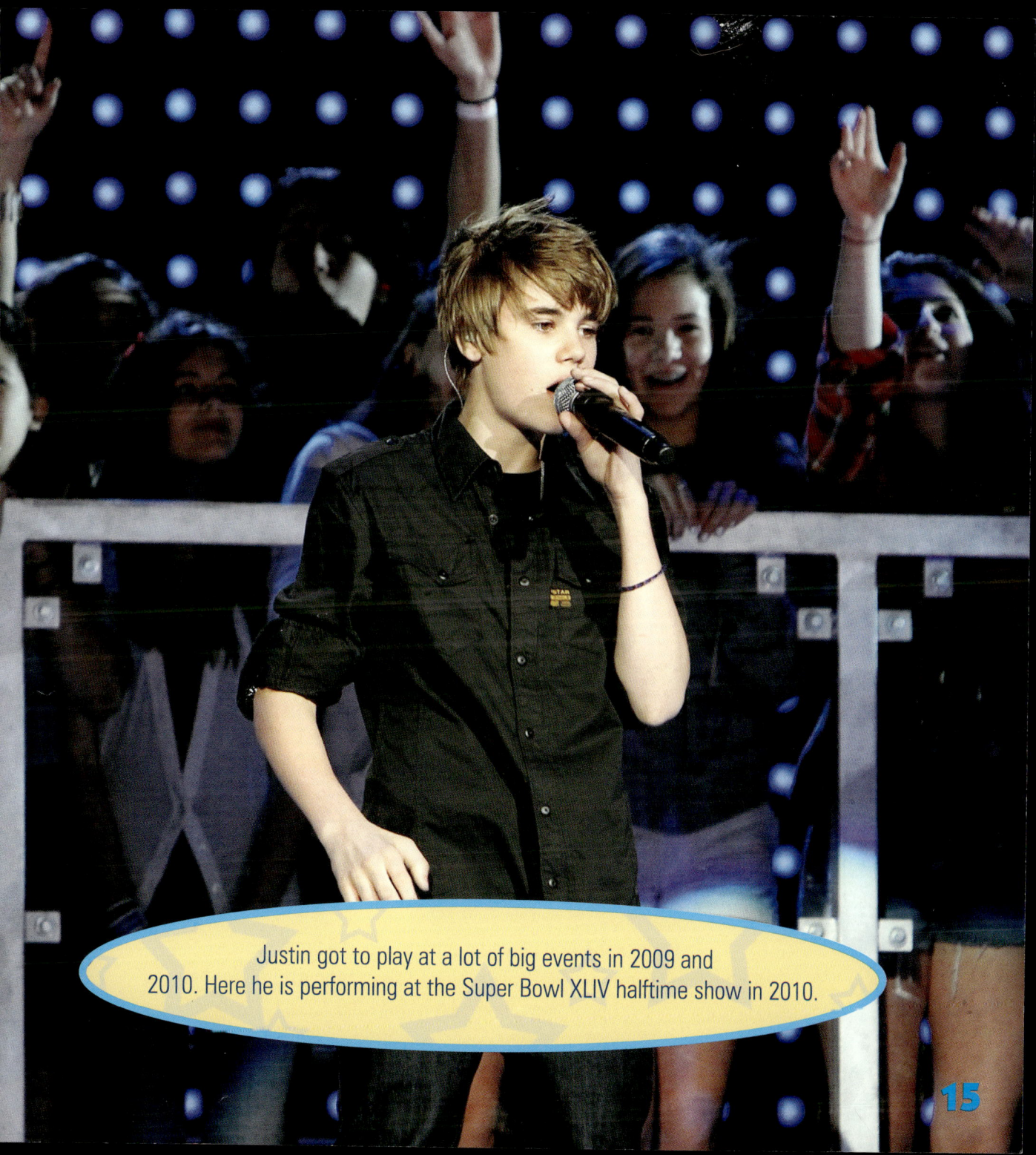

Justin got to play at a lot of big events in 2009 and 2010. Here he is performing at the Super Bowl XLIV halftime show in 2010.

15

Justin sang and played guitar on *Good Morning America* in November 2010. This helped keep fans excited for his upcoming album, *My World 2.0*.

My World 2.0

In January 2010, Justin released his second album, *My World 2.0*, with the singles "Baby," "Somebody to Love," and "U Smile."

My World 2.0 **debuted**, or first appeared, on the *Billboard* magazine charts at number one. The *Billboard* charts list albums in order of how popular they are each week. The list is based on how many albums are sold and how often the songs are played on the radio. Justin's album also debuted at number one on the music charts in Canada, Ireland, Australia, and New Zealand.

Never Say Never

In February 2011, *Justin Bieber: Never Say Never* hit the theaters. It is a 3D movie about Justin and his rise to fame. It includes performances from his US tour, along with some of his early YouTube videos, home videos, and scenes from his busy life.

Along with the film, Justin released an album of remixes, or new versions of his popular songs. The album is called *Never Say Never: The Remixes*. The title single, "Never Say Never," was the theme song for the 2010 movie *The Karate Kid*.

Justin Bieber: Never Say Never was released in 3D. Here, Usher, Justin, and Scooter Braun are wearing the special 3D glasses needed to see that special effect.

Justin is often seen with his girlfriend, actress and singer Selena Gomez. Here is the couple at an event in Hollywood in February 2011.

20

Bieber Offstage

Being a superstar is not always easy. There are people who do not like Justin's music very much, and they write about why they do not like it. For everyone who does not like him, though, Justin has many more fans.

More than 5 million people read his posts on the social networking Web site Twitter. That is nothing compared to the more than 26 million people who are fans of his Facebook page! His fans are what keep Justin excited about making music and touring. As Justin said in an interview with MTV, "At the end of the day, my fans are my everything."

FUN FACTS

★ When *My World* was released in 2009, it first appeared at number six on the *Billboard* magazine sales charts.

★ Justin has sold more than 4.5 million copies of his albums *My World*, *My World 2.0*, and *My Worlds Acoustic* worldwide. His singles have been downloaded from iTunes more than 10 million times.

★ In 2011, Justin was chosen by *Time* magazine as one of the 100 most influential people in the world.

★ In 2011, Justin won the Kids' Choice Award for Favorite Male Artist, and his song "Baby" won Favorite Song.

★ In March 2011, a wax statue of Justin Bieber was added to the other wax statues in Madame Tussauds museum in London, England.

★ In July 2010, Justin Bieber was the most searched for star on the Internet.

★ On September 23, 2010, and February 17, 2011, Justin played a guest role on the television crime show *CSI: Crime Scene Investigation*.

★ When Justin cut his hair in February 2011, pieces of his hair sold on the Web site eBay for $40,668. The money was given to a charity that helps animals.

★ Justin has put his name on nail polish, creating a One Less Lonely Girl collection for Nicole by OPI nail polish. The money from sales of the nail polish goes to help Pencils of Promise, a charity that builds schools.

★ Justin loves Canadian donut cha Tim Hortons!

Glossary

busking (BUSK-ing) Playing music in public for free or for spare change.

career (kuh-REER) A job.

debuted (DAY-byood) Had a first public appearance.

manager (MA-nih-jer) The person in charge of a performer.

music producers (MYOO-zik pruh-DOO-serz) People who record and put together records.

performance (per-FAWR-ments) The giving of a show.

platinum (PLAT-num) Describing an album that has sold more than one million copies.

promote (pruh-MOHT) Raised attention or awareness about something.

recording deal (rih-KAWR-ding DEEL) An agreement between a record label and an artist, in which the artist agrees to make recordings that the label will sell and promote.

released (ree-LEESD) Put out.

talent (TA-lent) A natural ability or skill.

viral (VY-rul) Having to do with a video on the Internet that becomes very popular quickly.

Index

A
album(s), 13, 17–18, 22

C
charm, 5
charts, 17, 22

F
fans, 5, 14, 21

G
guitar, 5–6

I
Island Records, 10, 13

M
music, 5, 21
music producers, 13

R
recording deal, 10
remixes, 18

S
sound, 5
superstar(s), 5, 21

V
video(s), 9–10, 18

Web Sites

Due to the changing nature of Internet links, PowerKids Press has developed an online list of Web sites related to the subject of this book. This site is updated regularly. Please use this link to access the list:
www.powerkidslinks.com/kids/bieber/